FUN FACT FILE: SPORTS!

20 FUN FACTS ABOUT BASKETBALL

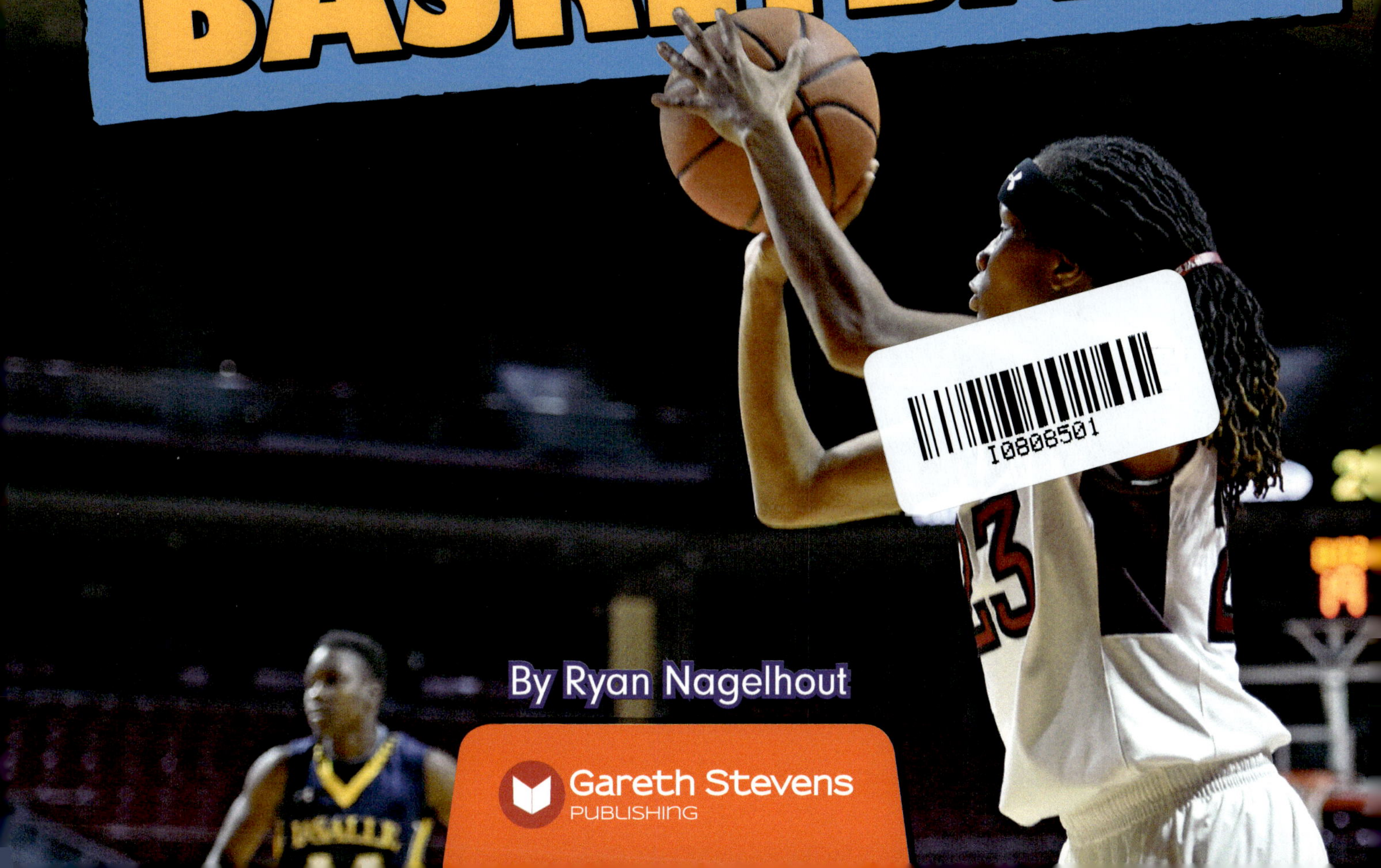

By Ryan Nagelhout

Gareth Stevens
PUBLISHING

Please visit our website, www.garethstevens.com. For a free color catalog of all our high-quality books, call toll free 1-800-542-2595 or fax 1-877-542-2596.

Cataloging-in-Publication Data

Nagelhout, Ryan.
20 fun facts about basketball / by Ryan Nagelhout.
p. cm. — (Fun fact file: sports!)
Includes index.
ISBN 978-1-4824-3969-4 (pbk.)
ISBN 978-1-4824-3970-0 (6-pack)
ISBN 978-1-4824-3973-1 (library binding)
1. Basketball — Juvenile literature. 2. Basketball — Miscellanea — Juvenile literature. I. Nagelhout, Ryan. II. Title.
GV885.1 N34 2016
796.323—d23

First Edition

Published in 2016 by
Gareth Stevens Publishing
111 East 14th Street, Suite 349
New York, NY 10003

Designer: Sarah Liddell
Editor: Ryan Nagelhout

Photo credits: Cover, p. 1 Aspen Photo/Shutterstock.com; pp. 5, 6 Hulton Archive/Staff/Hulton Archive/Getty Images; p. 7 Viscontino/Wikimedia Commons; p. 8 FREDERIC J. BROWN/Staff/AFP/Getty Images; p. 9 Thearon W. Henderson/Contributor/Getty Images Sport/Getty Images; pp. 10, 11 (background) Manny Millan/Contributor/Sports Illustrated/Getty Images; p. 11 (map) JUN KAWAGUCHI/Shutterstock.com; p. 12 Evadb/Wikimedia Commons; p. 13 Halvorsen brian/Wikimedia Commons; pp. 14, 21 (left) Focus On Sport/Contributor/Focus On Sport/Getty Images; p. 15 (Jerry West) George Long/Contributor/Sports Illustrated/Getty Images; p. 15 (logo) dean bertoncelj/Shutterstock.com; p. 16 Chris Covatta/Stringer/Getty Images Sport/Getty Images; p. 17 (background) Aksonov/E+/Getty Images; p. 18 Gibbsyspin/Wikimedia Commons; p. 19 Tony Tomsic/Contributor/WireImage/Getty Images; p. 20 Stephen Dunn/Staff/Getty Images Sport/Getty Images; p. 21 (right) Damian Strohmeyer/Contributor/Sports Illustrated/Getty Images; p. 22 TonyTheTiger/Wikimedia Commons; p. 23 Orlando Sentinel/Contributor/Tribune News Source/Getty Images; p. 24 Mitchell Layton/Contributor/Getty Images Sport/Getty Images; p. 25 JoeJohnson2/Wikimedia Commons; p. 26 Jonathan Daniel/Staff/Getty Images Sport/Getty Images; p. 27 Christian Petersen/Staff/Getty Images Sport/Getty Images; p. 29 Anadolu Agency/Contributor/Andolu Agency/Getty Images.

Printed in the United States of America

CPSIA compliance information: Batch #CW16GS: For further information contact Gareth Stevens, New York, New York at 1-800-542-2595.

Contents

Words in the glossary appear in **bold** type the first time they are used in the text.

History of Hoops

Unlike many other sports, the history of basketball is clear. In the winter of 1891–1892, Dr. James Naismith, a teacher at the YMCA in Springfield, Massachusetts, invented an **indoor** game that could be played between football and baseball seasons. Called "basket ball," his students took to it right away.

Basketball has become much more than a winter sport—more than 450 million people around the world play the game! Today the National Basketball **Association** (NBA) is the top men's league in the world, with teams in the United States and Canada.

Dr. James Naismith

Women also have a pro basketball league, the Women's National Basketball Association (WNBA).

First Shots

FACT 1

The first game of "basket ball" had 13 rules!

The game was played with soccer balls. Nine players were on each team until 1897, when it was changed to five. Hitting the ball with your fist was a foul! Dribbling the ball wasn't allowed yet. It wasn't in the rules!

James Naismith with his first basketball team

Naismith tried games with different numbers of players, but settled on nine for each team because he usually had 18 students in his class!

FACT 2

The first baskets were made for peaches!

In early basketball games, when a basket was scored, the game was stopped and a ladder was brought out to get the ball out of the peach basket. A hole was later cut into the bottom of the baskets so they didn't have to stop the game.

The baskets were hung 10 feet (3 m) off the ground, the same **height** nets hang from today.

On the Ball

FACT 3

Nonleather basketballs were a flop in the NBA.

In 2006, the league changed to **synthetic** balls made of fibers that didn't need to be broken in. The balls stuck to players' hands and often stuck between the rim and backboard. These balls were used for only 2 months before the NBA switched back to leather basketballs.

Phoenix Suns point guard Steve Nash even had to wear bandages on his fingers when he played because the synthetic balls kept cutting his hands!

leather game ball

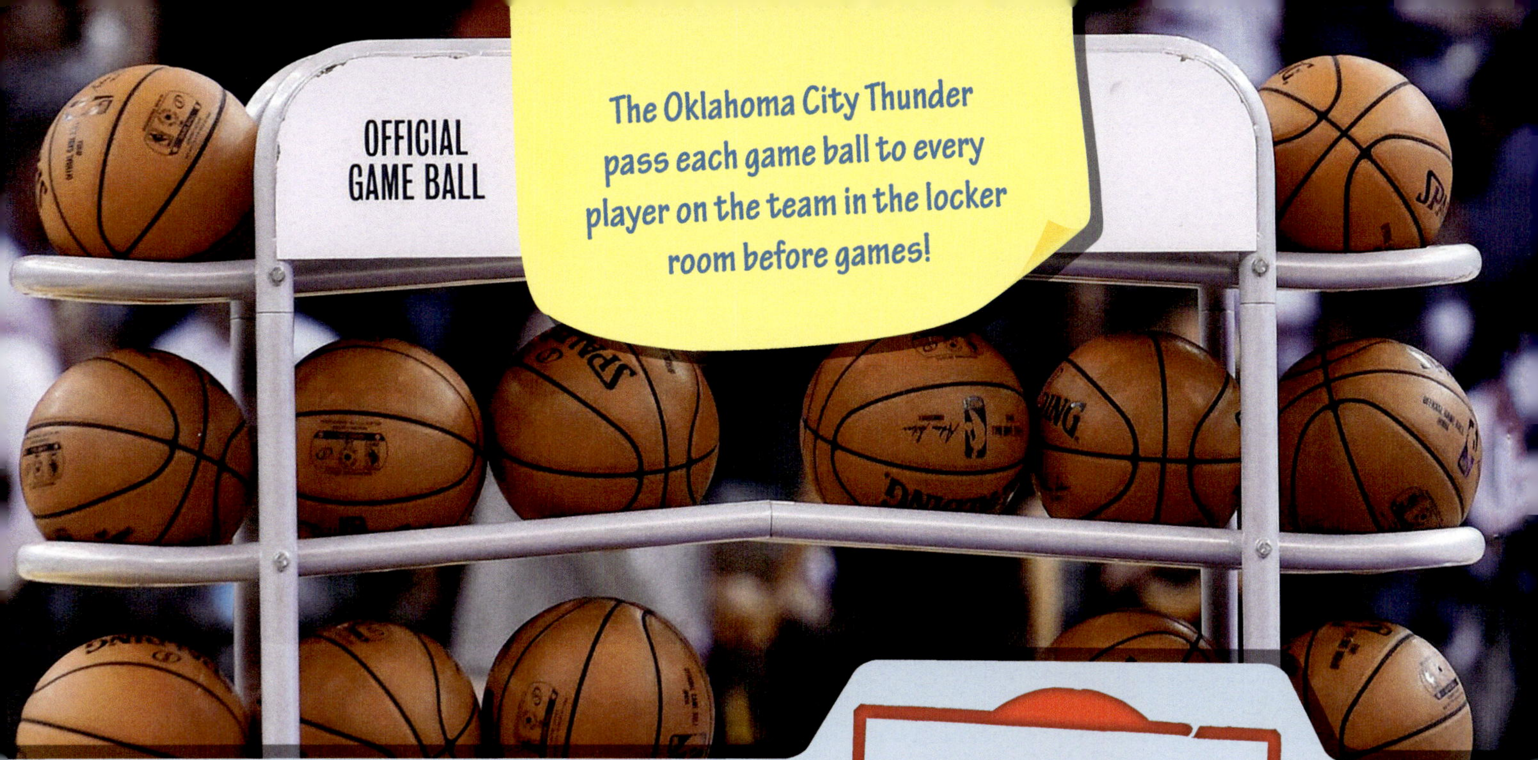

The Oklahoma City Thunder pass each game ball to every player on the team in the locker room before games!

FACT 4

NBA players get to test three "game balls" before every game.

One player from each team gets to try out leather basketballs and pick their favorites. The three balls both teams like are used in the game. Some players even smell basketballs to pick their game balls!

The Leagues

FACT 5

The NBA is made up of many different leagues!

The NBA was formed in 1949 when the Basketball Association of America (BAA) and the National Basketball League (NBL) **merged** after **competing** for 3 years. In 1976, four teams from the American Basketball Association joined the NBA when the ABA folded.

Two ABA teams—the Spirits of St. Louis and Kentucky Colonels—were bought out and their players were **drafted** by NBA teams.

The NBA/ABA Merger

This map shows what happened to the teams in the NBA and ABA when the two leagues merged in 1976.

Philadelphia vs San Antonio

FACT 6

The NBA once had a team in Sheboygan, Wisconsin!

In 1950, the NBA was just 17 teams in some smaller cities. The state of Indiana had three teams—the Fort Wayne Pistons, Anderson Packers, and Indianapolis Olympians. The Tri-Cities Blackhawks were one team for three cities: Moline, Illinois; Rock Island, Illinois; and Davenport, Iowa.

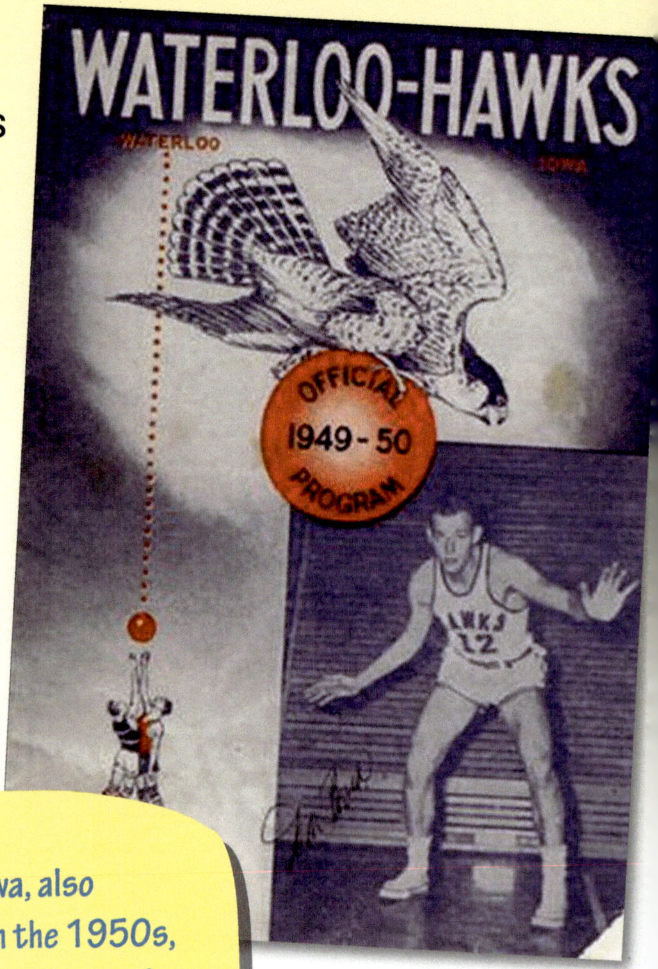

Waterloo, Iowa, also had an NBA team in the 1950s, as did the New York cities of Rochester and Syracuse.

FACT 7

Both Los Angeles teams have kept the nicknames from the cities their franchise used to play in.

The LA Lakers moved from Minneapolis, Minnesota, in 1960. The "Lakers" name is a reference to the many lakes in the state of Minnesota. The LA Clippers were moved from the coastal city of San Diego in 1984. A "clipper" is a fast sailboat.

The Clippers moved to San Diego in 1978 from Buffalo, New York, where the team was first called the Braves.

FACT 8

The Boston Celtics and Buffalo Braves once traded entire teams!

In 1978, Braves owner John Y. Brown and Celtics owner Irving H. Levin swapped franchises! Levin wanted to move a team west and thought moving the Braves—an **expansion team** just 8 years old—would be easier.

The franchise swap was even weirder because the teams made a 6-player trade after they traded owners!

Jerry West

FACT 9

The figure in the NBA logo is a real person!

The figure of Lakers legend Jerry West became the NBA logo in 1969. Artist Alan Siegel found a photo of West dribbling down the court and modeled his logo after it. He said it was West to a newspaper in 2010.

The NBA won't actually say it's West on "The Logo" because they might have to pay him to use his image!

Shooting from Downtown

FACT 10

The 3-point shot wasn't added to the NBA game until 1979!

The American Basketball League added the 3-point shot in 1961. Since then, the 3-point line has moved back several times and now sits 22 feet (6.7 m) from the hoop in the corners and 23 feet 9 inches (7.2 m) on the **arc**.

An early 3-point line sat just 19 feet (5.8 m) from the basket!

The 3-Point Line

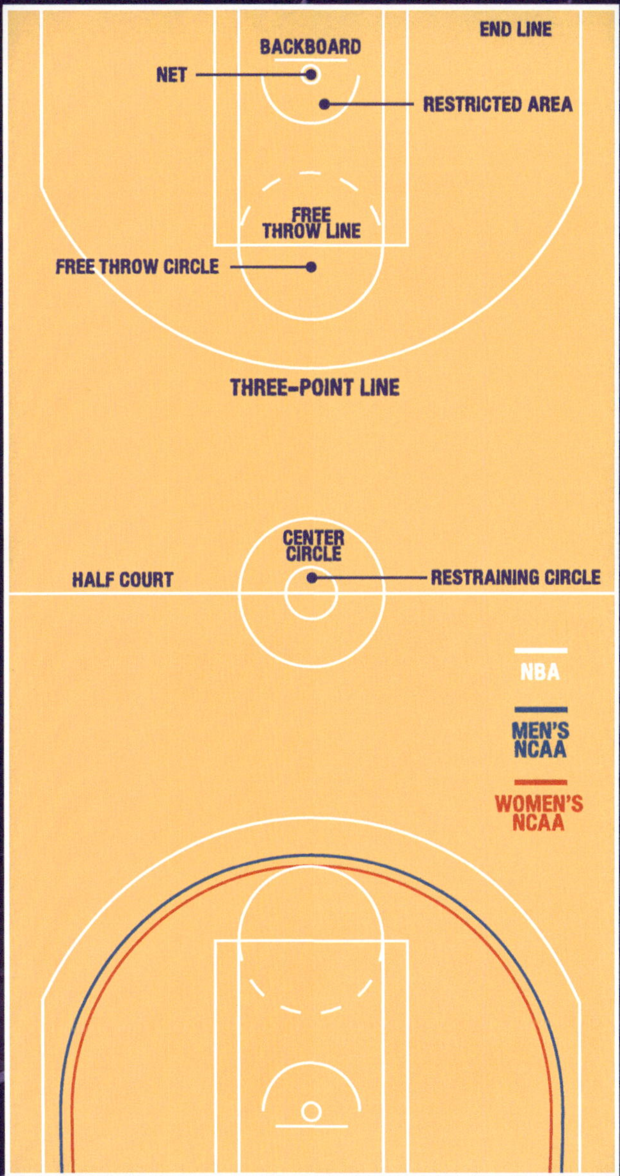

Here are the different 3-point lines in the men's and women's pro and college games.

Wilt's Wonders

FACT 11

Wilt the Stilt once scored 100 points in a game—by himself!

Wilt Chamberlain scored exactly 100 points while playing for the Philadelphia Warriors in 1962. Chamberlain made 36 shots from the field and hit 28 free throws in a 169-147 win over the New York Knicks on March 2.

Just 4,124 people saw the game where Chamberlain scored 100 points, which was played in Hershey, Pennsylvania.

FACT 12

Chamberlain never fouled out of a game in his 14-year career!

The 7-foot-1-inch center once said "nobody likes Goliath," but he played 1,045 regular season and 160 playoff games in his career without fouling out. That's 55,418 total minutes without ever picking up a sixth, and final, foul!

Chamberlain once wanted to try out for the US Olympic volleyball team, but wasn't allowed to because of his pro status in basketball.

Player Tales

FACT 13

A hurricane—and sharks—made NBA great Tim Duncan play basketball!

Duncan grew up in St. Croix, US Virgin Islands. He was a great swimmer who was training for the Olympics until a storm destroyed the only Olympic-sized pool on the island. He turned to hoops and became a two-time NBA Most **Valuable** Player (MVP)!

Duncan couldn't practice swimming in the ocean because he was scared of sharks!

Bol shares the record of tallest player ever with Gheorghe Muresan. Bol's the only player in history to have more blocks (2,086) than points scored (1,599)!

FACT 14

The shortest and tallest players in NBA history were on the same team!

During the 1987–1988 season, Manute Bol played on the Washington Bullets with Muggsy Bogues. Bol was a 7-foot-7-inch center and the tallest player in NBA history. Bogues, meanwhile, was the shortest player in the league at 5 feet 3 inches.

Taking Shots

FACT 15

The 24-second shot clock came from a math problem!

The shot clock was added in 1954 by Syracuse Nationals owner Danny Biasone. He noticed teams in high-scoring games took about 60 shots a game. He **divided** the length of a game—48 minutes (2,880 seconds)—by 120 shots and got 24 seconds each shot.

The shot clock was added to stop teams from stalling with the ball. Some teams held on to the ball for minutes on end!

FACT 16

In 1950, the Fort Wayne Pistons beat the Minneapolis Lakers, 19-18!

The lowest-scoring game in NBA history saw Fort Wayne outscore the Lakers 3-1 in the fourth quarter. The lowest-scoring game in the shot-clock era was between the Celtics and Hawks. The Celtics won, 62-57, in 1955.

In 2015, the New York Knicks and Orlando Magic played the lowest-scoring quarter. The Knicks outscored the Magic, 8-7!

FACT 17

The Miami Heat once lost by 68 points!

On December 17, 1991, the Cleveland Cavaliers beat the Heat, 148-80, at home. Eight Heat players had at least 11 points in the game. The Heat were led by Steve Smith, who had 15 points.

Steve Smith

Despite that terrible game, the Heat finished 38-44 on the season and actually made the playoffs!

FACT 18

The NBA championship trophy changed in 1984.

The original NBA Finals trophy was named after former Celtics owner Walter A. Brown in 1949. In 1984, a new trophy was made. Named after NBA **commissioner** Larry O'Brien, the trophy has been given to the league champion every year since.

The winning team gets to keep the trophy. It costs $13,500 to make a new trophy every year!

FACT 19

Diana Taurasi won four straight WNBA scoring titles.

Taurasi won her first scoring title with the Phoenix Mercury in 2006. The first overall pick in the 2004 WNBA draft then won the league scoring crown from 2008 to 2011! She won the league's Most Valuable Player award during the 2008–2009 season.

Taurasi and the Mercury won the WNBA title in 2007, 2009, and 2014.

Thompson is the only player in WNBA history to have more than 7,000 points and 3,000 rebounds.

FACT 20

Tina Thompson leads the WNBA in all-time scoring.

Thompson was the first overall pick in the first WNBA draft in 1997. She played for three teams—the Houston Comets, Los Angeles Sparks, and Seattle Storm—during her 17-year WNBA career and finished with 7,488 points.

More to Learn

There's lots more history hidden in basketball. Teams have moved all over the country over the years. Did you know the Denver Nuggets were once called the Larks and Rockets at different times?

Some teams disappeared, only to have new ones take their place. Many players—Chucky Brown and Jim Jackson to name a few—have suited up for a dozen NBA teams in their careers. Did you know Drew Gooden played for 10 different teams in 12 seasons? As each season passes, the league creates more hoops history. That means there are many more fun basketball facts to discover!

Drew Gooden

Gooden has played for Memphis, Orlando, Cleveland, Chicago, Sacramento, San Antonio, Dallas, the Los Angeles Clippers, Milwaukee, and Washington in his career!

Glossary

arc: part of a curved line

association: a group with common interests

commissioner: the person in charge of a league

compete: to try to win a contest with others

divide: to find out how many times one number fits into another number

draft: to pick players for a team. Also, the act of picking players for a team.

expansion team: a team newly added to the league

franchise: a team that's part of a certain league

height: the distance measured from the bottom to the top of something

indoor: having to do with the inside of a building

merge: to come together

synthetic: made not of natural matter

trophy: a prize given for winning

valuable: having a lot of skill that helps a team

For More Information

Books

Graubart, Norman D. *The Science of Basketball.* New York, NY: PowerKids Press, 2016.

Omoth, Tyler. *Who's Who of Pro Basketball: A Guide to the Game's Greatest Players.* North Mankato, MN: Capstone Press, 2016.

Winters, Jaime. *Ruling the Court: Basketball's Biggest Wins.* New York, NY: Crabtree Publishing, 2016.

Websites

Basketball Basics
hooptactics.com/Basketball_Basics_Original_Basketball_Rules
Read all 13 of the original rules of basketball here, and see how the game has changed.

Basketball Reference
basketball-reference.com
Discover more stats and figures about your favorite ABA and NBA players here.

National Basketball Association
nba.com
Find out more about players and teams in the NBA on the league's official site.

Publisher's note to educators and parents: Our editors have carefully reviewed these websites to ensure that they are suitable for students. Many websites change frequently, however, and we cannot guarantee that a site's future contents will continue to meet our high standards of quality and educational value. Be advised that students should be closely supervised whenever they access the Internet.

Index